Story Time

Written by: H. Shain
Translated and adapted by: Bahtya Minkin
Illustrated by: G.P.

Originally published in Hebrew as *She'at Sipur*
Pe'er Publishers, 2004. Graphic Design by Ben Gasner Studio

ISBN 978-1-59826-909-3

Pe'er Publishers, Israel
03-618-1129

Translated and adapted by Bahtya Minkin
Graphic Design by Bat-Chen Grossman
Illustrations by G.P.

Table of Contents

Introduction

Preschool children will enjoy the fourteen entrancing stories in *Story Time* which will turn story time into an enriching, enjoyable, exciting experience. Clear, easy-to-read language, along with world-famous G.P.'s vivid, full-color illustrations, make this book the perfect choice to read to young children.

Story Time was edited by child-development specialists in order to join pleasure with learning, an exciting experience with amassing knowledge, *chinuch* and encouragement with lots of happiness and laughter.

In order to enjoy the complete scope of benefits this book has to offer, keep in mind that the following can be developed during story time:

1. Teaching Torah values

A good story time provides a child with an important, and pleasurable, emotional experience. The child becomes a partner in the story, and absorbs subtle messages and values. The values that come across through the story are very powerful and will accompany the child throughout his life.

An effort was made to stress values such as *emunah*, good *middos*, sharing, respecting others, gratitude, welcoming guests, *hashavas aveidah*, and more.

2. Parent-child bonding

A comfortable story-time session, when parent and child are sitting close together, is an excellent way to strengthen their emotional bond. Take advantage of these wonderful moments together to strengthen your bond with your child. Listen to what he has to say and let him choose which story to read. Don't force him to "stay on the same page" as you, even if you haven't finished reading that page or working with the skills addressed there.

3. Language development

When reading to a child, you are introducing him to a wide vocabulary and the word structure of both new and familiar words. He is exposed to various writing styles and learns new words. He learns about rhyming and word games, as well as expressions and proper communication.

When choosing a story to read to your child, it's important to choose one that is a step above his current spoken language skills. These stories were written in a light, easy-to-understand style, yet the words are rich and varied. It's advisable to read these stories as they are, to get your child used to the written language. When you reach a hard word, read it, and then explain it immediately. This will give your child the opportunity to learn new words without losing interest in the story.

This activity, transitioning between the spoken language and the written word, is one of the most important steps of reading-readiness.

4. Acquiring literary comprehension and love of reading

When a child discovers the written word and begins to enjoy reading, he acquires an awareness of the power hidden in the written word, and this will motivate him to read on his own. In addition, the young child will acquire basic literary comprehension, he will recognize the structure of a story, and will develop a sensitivity and expectation to discover similar structures in future stories that he reads.

5. Reading-readiness development

Parents who read to their children from a young age are developing their children's perception that the message of the story is transmitted via the written word, and not via illustrations. These children will attempt to make a connection between the words they see with the sounds of the ABC, which are familiar to them from everyday speech.

This is an imperative stage of the reading process, and that's why it's important for parents to keep their finger on the place as they read aloud. This is another way for a child to acquire reading-readiness skills: he will be able to point to a word or two, and in time, he will also begin to understand the role of punctuation marks.

6. Phonics development

Phonics awareness is when a child is aware of the word's sound structure. (For example, the word "telephone" is made up of three syllables: te-le-phone.) Practicing phonics awareness has a profound impact on the reading process. In order to develop phonics awareness, it's important to read rhymes with your child and to let him fill in the missing rhyme himself. The stories in *Story Time* were written in rich rhyme, with varied sounds, to give children the opportunity to practice this important skill. While reading to your child, it's advised to include him in filling in rhyming words and sentences.

7. Cognitive and motor development

Story Time will assist in your child's cognitive development, including: comprehension, logic, visual-and audio-memory, visual- and audio-conception and identifying the unbelievable. It can also assist in the following areas of motor development: strengthening hand-eye coordination, and spatial ability.

Reading the stories in *Story Time* and completing the accompanying activities with your child will assist you in cultivating many talents that are important for your child's development.

8. Problem-solving skills

When a storyline reflects your child's own feelings and emotions, your child will relate to the problem and will learn how to deal with it effectively. He will learn how to let go of negative feelings, cultivate positive emotions and internalize messages.

9. Reading for beginners

The structure and style of this book lends itself to being not just a "read-aloud" book, but also a "read-along" book, which beginning readers will be able to read to themselves.

A child who is in the process of learning how to read is not considered an actual "reader" as long as he doesn't understand what he's reading — even if he can read the words perfectly.

This book will motivate your child to understand the text: the stories are written clearly, the rhyming text is fun to read and listen to, and the vivid, detailed illustrations will stimulate your child to read and understand.

Wishing you an enjoyable, exciting experience, and hoping you derive many hours of quality story time,
Pe'er Publishers

A Gift That Lasts

Yossi's mother gave him
A wonderful thing.
A big blue balloon
On a long, long string.

With his brand-new present
Held tight in his fist,
He ran out to see how
It would bounce, float,
and twist.

He tugged on the string.
The balloon jumped
and danced.
It sailed through the air
Whenever he ran.
But suddenly, the wind,
With a blustery gust,
Blew it into a tree branch
And caused it to bust.

Yossi came to his mother,
Looking downcast.
"Why do you look so sad?"
Mommy asked.
"My balloon popped,"
said Yossi,
As he started to cry.
"Don't worry,"
said his mother,
"And I'll tell you why!
When your birthday comes,
You will get a surprise!"

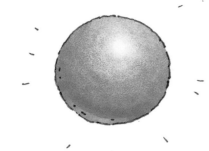

When Yossi's birthday came,
The surprise that he got
Was a big purple ball,
And he liked it a lot!
He took it outside
To play, and he called
To his friends, "Hey, guys!
Look at my new ball!"

"Throw it high!" They all yelled.
"Throw it hard! Throw it fast!"
So Yossi did just
As his friends had all asked.
He tossed it up high,
But he threw it so hard
That the ball bounced
Down the stairs
And out of the yard.

Yossi searched and searched
for his ball.
But it was gone.
He couldn't find it at all.

Yossi came to his mother,
Looking downcast.
"Why do you look so sad?"
Mommy asked.
"I lost my ball," Yossi said,
As he started to cry.
"Don't worry," said his mother,
"And I'll tell you why!
When Chanukah comes,
You will get a surprise!"

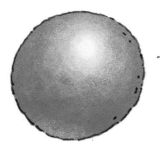

Chanukah came
And to Yossi's delight,
He was given a present
On the very first night.
A toy car, with doors
That could open and close,
With wheels that spun quickly,
And lights on its nose.

He ran to play in his room
With the car that he got.
He built a crosswalk with signs
And a big parking lot.
He made the car turn left,
He made it turn right.
He made it zoom
Through his room
That first Chanukah night.

But with a crash and a crunch,
Yossi saw with dismay
That his car was not built
To be played with that way.
It crashed into the wall
And was scraped on the floor.
Now a wheel had come off,
And he couldn't open the door.

Yossi came to his mother,
Looking downcast.
"Why do you look so sad?"
Mommy asked.
"My car broke," said Yossi,
As he started to cry.
"Don't worry," said his mother.
"And I'll tell you why!
    When Rosh Chodesh comes,
      You will get a surprise!"

On Rosh Chodesh,
Mommy, just as she said,
Gave Yossi some stickers:
Blue, purple, and red.
And many other colors,
Like yellow and green –
The prettiest stickers
Yossi had ever seen.

He got right to work,
Putting stickers around
The edge of a large
Piece of paper he found.
Then in the middle,
He made a big face
With eyes, nose, and a mouth.
And he left plenty of space.

He wanted to make
A body below.
But when he reached for his
stickers,
He realized with woe
That the stickers were gone!
He had used every one.
He could not continue.
No stickers. No fun.

Yossi came to his mother,
Looking downcast.
"Why do you look so sad?"
Mommy asked.
"No more stickers," Yossi said,
As he started to cry.
"Don't worry," said his mother.
"And I'll tell you why!
When Pesach comes
You will get a surprise!"

As Pesach came closer,
Mommy went to the store,
And told the saleswoman
What she was looking for.

"I have just the thing!"
The saleswoman replied.
"A new book just came out.
It's called *Story Time*!"

Yossi's mother took a look,
And liked what she saw.
So she bought the book.

She gave it to Yossi
That very afternoon,
And he took it upstairs
To read in his room.

Now Yossi reads *Story Time*
Every night.
The stories are fun,
And the pictures are bright.

And the very best thing
Is that a book doesn't pop,
It doesn't get lost
And it can't get used up.
It's a gift that will last.
It won't burst or bend.

A book is forever.
A book is a friend.

The Helpful Fruits and Vegetables

Once there was a lemon,
A pepper, an orange,
An apple, and a strawberry.

They went for a walk
Together one day.
Jumping and skipping
Along the way.

They met a small boy
With some tea in a mug,
And a scarf 'round his neck,
Tied up warm and snug.

They asked the boy, "Are you okay?
Why aren't you in school today?"

"I wish I could go to school today,
But I have a sore throat," he replied with dismay.

Suddenly, the lemon
Ran forward, jumped up,
And said, "Take me,
And squeeze me into your cup!
Hashem made me
With the ability
To make your throat feel better
If you drink me."

The boy agreed,
And the lemon stayed.
The pepper, the orange,
The apple, and the strawberry
Went on their way.

With a jump and a hop,
With a bounce and a twist,
They went searching for more
People to assist.

They walked through the playground.
Girls were laughing and singing.
Playing jump rope,
Running, sliding, and swinging.

But one girl was sitting
On the side, on a stone.
She wasn't playing with anyone.
She was sitting alone.

They asked the girl, "Why don't you play?
Why are you sitting alone on this beautiful day?"

"I'm very tired," the girl replied.
"I don't have the strength to jump and slide."

Suddenly, the pepper
Ran forward, jumped up,
And said, "Make a *bracha*
And eat me all up!
Hashem made me
With the ability
To give you energy
If you eat me!"

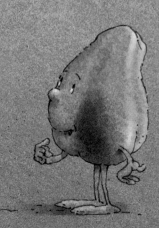

The girl agreed,
And the pepper stayed.
The orange, the apple, and the strawberry
Went on their way.

With a jump and a hop,
With a bounce and a twist,
They went searching for more
People to assist.

On the side of the street
They saw a man
In raggedy clothes
Holding out his hand.

"How sad!" said the apple.
"That man is so poor
He can't even buy food
In the grocery store."

Said the apple to the poor man:
"Would you like something to eat?
I'm juicy and filling.
A nice, tasty treat.
Hashem made me
With the ability
To fill up your belly
If you eat me!"

The poor man agreed,
And the apple stayed.
The orange and strawberry
Went on their way.

With a jump and a hop,
With a bounce and a twist,
They went searching for more
People to assist.

The mailman was on
The road up ahead.
His nose was runny.
His eyes were all red.

He had a bag full of mail
That needed delivery
But he was feeling so sick,
Headachy, and shivery.

"You don't look so good,"
The two fruits said.
"Your eyes are tearing.
Your nose is so red!"

"I can't do my job,"
The mailman answered back,
"'Cause each time I try to
Reach into my sack
My nose starts to run,
And my eyes start to tear.
I'm too sick to work
Today, I fear."

Suddenly, the orange
Ran forward, jumped up,
And said, "Please, take me!"
And eat me all up!
Hashem made me
With the ability
To cure your cold
If you eat me!"

The mailman agreed,
And the orange stayed.
The strawberry continued,
Alone, on his way.

The strawberry realized
Each of his friends
Found a way to be useful,
And now at the end
Of their journey, the strawberry
Was all alone.
There was no one to help,
So he just went home.

At home, in the kitchen,
Mommy seemed sort of nervous.
"Can I help you?" asked the strawberry.
"I'm at your service."

"Today is Leah's birthday.
I made her a treat:
A cake with cream frosting,
Fluffy and sweet.
But now I need something
To place on the top.
Something pretty and bright
To finish it up."

"This cake will look great
With me in the middle!"
The strawberry said.
"And though I may be little,
I can be very useful!"
And with a skip and a hop
He ran up to the cake,

And he jumped right on top.

A Bib for Efraim

On Sunday, when Efraim sat down to eat,
His shirt was clean, his clothes were neat.
As he took his place upon his chair,
Mommy handed him a bib to wear.

"I don't need a bib," Efraim said sweetly.
"I'm a big boy. I can eat very neatly."
His place was set with a bowl, spoon, and cup.
His noodle soup was delicious!
He ate it all up.

After lunch, Mommy said:
"Who would like to come to the store with me?"
"I do!" Efraim replied, instantly.
But when he looked down—Oh!
What did he see?

A shirt full of noodle,
Soup stains, and more.
And Efraim knew he could not go to the store.
His shirt was too dirty. He just couldn't go.

So Mommy went shopping,
and Efraim stayed home.

On Monday, when Efraim sat down to eat,
Once again, his clothes were clean and neat.
He took his place upon his chair,
And Mommy handed him a bib to wear.

"I don't need a bib," Efraim said sweetly.
"I'm a big boy. I can eat very neatly."

His place was set with a plate, fork, and cup.
Lunch was meatballs and rice,
and he ate it all up.

After lunch, his big brother Chaim said:
"Who wants to come to the park with me?"
"I do!" Efraim replied, instantly.
But when he looked down—Oh!
What did he see?

Bits of rice! And tomato sauce stains!
And to Efraim it was quite plain
That he couldn't go to the park with Chaim.
So his big brother left, without Efraim.

On Tuesday, when Efraim sat down to eat,
His shirt was clean and his clothes were neat.
He took his place upon his chair,
And Mommy handed him a bib to wear.

"I don't need a bib," Efraim said sweetly.
"I'm a big boy. I can eat very neatly."

His place was set with a bowl, spoon, and cup.
Mashed potatoes and carrots: he ate them all up.

That evening, Abba said:
"Who wants to visit Zaidy with me?"
"I do!" Efraim replied, instantly.
But when he looked down—Oh! What did he see?

Orange spots on his shirt from the carrots he ate.
He wanted to go, but Abba couldn't wait.
"Zaidy will be so sad I'm not there,
But with a shirt this dirty, I can't go anywhere.

For the past three days, I couldn't do
All the fun things I wanted to.
Because my shirt always had a bunch
Of stains from the food I ate for lunch."

Efraim now knew that if he wanted to have fun
He'd have to be clean when lunch was done.
So from that day on, he always stayed neat
By wearing a bib when he sat down to eat.

23

The Goat Who Loved To Have Guests

Once upon a time a goat named Nanny lived in a beautiful house with many rooms — enough rooms to host many guests.

One morning...

Nanny heard footsteps on the path outside.
Who was coming? She opened the door wide.

It was Mrs. Cow, with a smile on her face.
"Nanny, my dear, can I stay at your place?
I can give you milk, butter, yogurt and cheese.
What do you say? Can I stay with you, please?"

"Of course!" Nanny said.
"Come in. Please do.
I love to have guests,
And I'd love to have you!"

And Nanny and Mrs. Cow,
I'm quite happy to tell
Lived happily together.
And all was well.

That afternoon....

Nanny and the cow
Heard footsteps outside.
Who was coming?
They opened the door wide.

It was Mrs. Hen, and she had a request.
"Can I stay here, Nanny? Can I be your guest?
Have you room in your house for me? If you do,
I'd be happy to share my eggs with you."

"Of course," Nanny said.
"Come in. Please do.
I love to have guests,
And I'd love to have you!"

And the goat, cow and hen,
I'm quite happy to tell,
Live happily together.
And all was well.

That evening...

Nanny, Mrs. Hen and Mrs. Cow
Heard footsteps outside.
Who was coming?
They opened the door wide.

There on the path stood Mrs. Sheep
And she said, "Do you have a place I can sleep?
If you have some room, and your house isn't full
I'd be happy to give you some of my wool!"

"Of course," Nanny said.
"Come in. Please do.
I love to have guests,
And I'd love to have you!"

And the sheep, hen, cow and goat
I'm quite happy to tell,
All lived happily together.
And all was well.

That night...

Nanny, Mrs. Cow, Mrs. Hen and Mrs. Sheep
Heard little footsteps on the path outside.
Who was coming? They opened the door wide.

It was Baby Chick, so frail and small.
She was shivering, and didn't look happy at all.
"Can I stay with you? I have no place to live.
But I'm sorry, I do not have anything to give."

Nanny's heart went out to the poor Baby Chick.
She couldn't just leave her outside to get sick!
"Of course! Come in! There's plenty of space.
For a Baby Chick, this is the perfect place.

Come eat, come drink! It's time we all learn
We don't need to get anything in return.
Having a guest is it's own reward!"
And the chick came inside.
And she was loved and adored.

She began to get better, she began to get stronger.
In a few weeks she was frail and small no longer.
And so, the chick and the sheep
The hen, goat and cow
Live in peace and friendship together, now.
With joy and with love, with jokes and with laughter,
They will all live happily ever after!

The Big Blue Car

A big blue car was completely stuck
In the middle of the road. Oh, what bad luck!
He had a flat tire. He was in a quite a pinch.
He could not move forward.
Not a smidge. Not an inch.

An ambulance with a flashing light
And painted all in red and white
Tried to drive through,
But he couldn't get past.
"What's the hold-up?"
The ambulance asked.
"Eli the Builder dropped a brick
On his foot, and now we need to go quick
To the hospital. He might need a cast.
Please get out of the way, and let me get past!"

And there in the road
The big blue car sat,
Trying to move despite his flat.
RUM RUM...RUM RUM!
He was in quite a pinch.
He could not move forward.
Not a smidge. Not an inch.

Soon, a red fire engine with a very long ladder
Stopped and looked up ahead to see what's the matter.
"WHEE-OO! WHEE-OO! What's this traffic about?
There's a fire in the field and I must put it out!
I need to spray water to douse all the flames.
I can't wait one more minute!" The fire engine exclaimed.

And there in the road
The big blue car sat,
Trying to move despite his flat.
RUM RUM...RUM RUM!
He was in quite a pinch.
He could not move forward.
Not a smidge. Not an inch.

Along came a garbage truck who was on his way
To collect all the garbage from the town that day.
"HONK HONK...HONK HONK! Let me get by.
My job is important, and I'll tell you why.
If I can't collect garbage, the whole town, I guess
Will be very smelly! A big, dirty mess!"

And there in the road
The big blue car sat,
Trying to move despite his flat.
RUM RUM...RUM RUM!
He was in quite a pinch.
He could not move forward.
Not a smidge. Not an inch.

34

At the end of the line, a schoolbus stood.
He said, "This traffic is not good!
These children will be late for class
If I do not find a way to pass!"
BEEP! BEEP! BEEP!
He honked his horn loud.
But no one heard him
Among the crowd.

And there in the road
The big blue car sat,
Trying to move despite his flat.
RUM RUM...RUM RUM!
He was in quite a pinch.
He could not move forward.
Not a smidge. Not an inch.

And then....FINALLY!

The tow truck showed up
And with a big hook he towed
That poor broken car
To the side of the road.

The street was now clear!
Everyone could get through
And go do all the jobs
They needed to do!

WHEE-OO! WHEE-OO! The fire engine said,
As he drove to catch up with the ambulance ahead.
BEEP! BEEP! HONK! HONK! Said the bus and the truck.
They were all so happy to no longer be stuck!

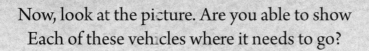

Now, look at the picture. Are you able to show
Each of these vehicles where it needs to go?

Whose Ball Is This?

Teddy went out to his garden one day
To pick some flowers, and to play.
And there in the weeds near the fence was a ball
That did not belong to him at all.

"Whoever lost this must miss it," he thought.
"And I'll find the owner, just like I was taught.
Returning lost objects is a very good deed."
And he ran off to do just that—at top speed.

Teddy Bear decided to make a sign.
He wrote it carefully, line by line.

LOST AND FOUND
Please knock on my door
or give me a call
If you have
lost a ball.

KNOCK, KNOCK, KNOCK!
"Who's there?" Teddy called.
"It's Miss String of Beads—about that ball!"
In walked a string of colored beads,
Looking very sad indeed.
She said:
"I've lost the last bead from my string.
Is that what you found? Is that the thing?
It was round and purple and sparkles bright
It slipped from my string 'cause the knot wasn't tight."

"I'm sorry," said Teddy.
"That's not what I found
In my garden, on the ground.
The ball I found was
blue, orange, and red.
But I sure hope you find
your lost bead," he said.

KNOCK, KNOCK, KNOCK!
"Who's there?" Teddy called.
"It's Mrs. Egg—about that ball!"
Teddy opened the door. Mrs. Egg stood there.
"Oh, Teddy," she sobbed, "I've looked everywhere!
It's my yolk! It's gone missing. I've looked all around.
Is my yellow yolk the ball you found?"

Teddy Bear sadly shook his head.
"I'm sorry. That's not the ball I found," he said.
"But I'm sure *someone* will find your yolk,"
And he smiled sincerely as he spoke.

KNOCK KNOCK, KNOCK!
"Who's there?" Teddy called.
"It's Miss Lollipop—about the ball!"
In she walked, looking quite odd
With no candy on top, just a wrapper wad.
"Have you seen my candy? It fell off my stick.
It's red and round and tasty to lick.
Is that the ball you found outside?
I really miss my candy," she sighed.
"Without that tasty ball on top
I'm not a lolly, I'm just a pop."

"How sad you lost your top!"
Teddy frowned.
"But yours is not the ball I found.
The one I found is not something to eat.
It's the kind that you bounce,
or kick with your feet."

Feeling discouraged, Teddy let out a sigh
And wondered if the ball's owner
would ever come by.
He sat in his garden, looking downcast.
"Will I *ever* find the ball's owner?" he asked.

43

KNOCK, KNOCK, KNOCK!
"Who's there?" Teddy called.
"It's me — Bina Bunny! — about the ball!
I was just walking by, and I noticed your sign,
And I think that ball you found might be mine!
I was playing near here, and I bounced it too hard.
I think it might have bounced into your yard.
I was so sad when I lost it. It's practically new.
When it bounced out of sight, I didn't know what to do.
Is the ball you found blue, orange, and red?
I'd be so happy to get my ball back," she said.

"Yes! Yes! That's the ball that I found! That's the one!
My search for the owner is finally done!
I'm so happy I get to return your lost ball.
Returning lost things is a *mitzvah*, after all."

And now, can you help Miss String of Beads,
Mrs. Egg, and Miss Lollipop find what they need?

Who Deserves the Thanks?

One morning, Uri awoke early and bright,
Refreshed after sleeping well all night.
He said *modeh ani* and quickly got dressed.
And as he stepped into the kitchen, Ima made a request.

"Uri, I need you to run to the store
And pick up some bread. We don't have any more."
So Uri ran down the block to Tasty n' Kosher
And bought a fresh loaf of bread from Nachum the grocer.

"Thank you, Mr. Grocer," little Uri said.
"Thank you very much for making this bread!"

"You're welcome, Uri.
You're so polite, and so kind.
But there is one thing that you
must keep in mind.
It's Shimon the truck driver
who brings me the bread.
All I do is sell it to you,"
Nachum said.

So out of the grocery store Uri ran
To find Shimon unloading his delivery van.
"Thank you, Mr. Truck Driver," Uri said.
"Thank you very much for making this bread!"

"You're welcome, Uri. You're so polite and so kind.
But there is one thing that you must keep in mind.
Eli the baker is the one who makes the bread.
I just deliver it to the stores," Shimon said.

So Uri ran to the bakery, where Eli was found
Making more loaves of bread, so fresh, soft and round.
"Thank you, Mr. Baker," little Uri said.
"Thank you so much for making this bread!"

"You're welcome. Uri. You're so polite and so kind.
But there is one thing that you must keep in mind.
The farmer is the one who spends hour after hour
Cutting and grinding the wheat to make flour.

Once all that work is done, I use that flour to make bread.
So the farmer is the one who works hardest," Eli said.

So out Uri ran, to a large field of wheat
Where he found Avi the farmer in the tractor seat.
"Thank you, Mr. Farmer," little Uri said.
"Thank you for making the flour for bread!"

"You're welcome, Uri. You're so polite and so kind.
But there is one thing that you must keep in mind.
I don't make the wheat. I just plant the seeds.
Then Hashem gives the plant everything else that it needs.

He makes the sun shine. He makes the rain fall.
And when the wheat is done growing, I just collect it all.
So don't thank me for that delicious bread.
Do you know who you should be thanking instead?"

"How can I thank Hashem?" Uri thought
As he ran home with the loaf of bread that he bought.

By the time Uri came home, he understood
There was a way to thank Hashem for his food.
He washed his hands carefully, and sat down at the table to
Say the very best "*hamotzi*" blessing that he was able to.

What Am I Made Of? Each of the foods in the column on the right was made from one of the foods in the column on the left. Can you match the foods together? What *bracha* do we make on each of these foods?

Where's My Brother?

-Hello, little boy. What's your name?

-Yochanan.

-Why are you crying, Yochanan?

-I was watching the boys play on the swings, and when I turned around, my big brother wasn't with me anymore.

-Don't worry. Tell me what your brother looks like, and we'll find him together.

Is your brother fat?

-No, nothing like that.

-Is your brother thin?

-Yes. He always has been.

-Is your brother short?

-No. He's not that sort.

-Is your brother tall?

-Yes! The tallest of all.

-Is your brother sad?

-No, he's usually glad.

-Does your brother smile?

-Yes. That's much more his style.

Can you find
Yochanan's brother?

Pick him out from
all the others.

56

The Bird and the Hen

One morning, a hen with a pretty red crest
Was approached by a little bird, during breakfast.
The little bird said, "I'm quite hungry today.
Perhaps you can spare some of your grain?"

"NO!" the hen shouted. "These seeds are mine!
I collected them myself and it took a long time!
If you're hungry and looking for something to eat
Go get your own food, with your own two feet."

"Fine!" the bird responded.
"If you don't want to share,
Eat it all by yourself, for all I care!"
And the poor little bird, hurt and offended
Turned around, flapped her wings,
And to the sky she ascended.

But suddenly, the hen started feeling bad
That she didn't share the seeds that she had.
"That poor little bird. She was hungry, in need.
And I wouldn't even give her one single seed!
I must catch up to her, and right my mistakes.
And I'm going to keep trying, no matter how long it takes!"

The hen jumped to her feet, and as fast as she could
She ran to catch up with the poor little bird.
She ran and she ran for a long, long while.
She ran and she ran, mile after mile.
She didn't stop running, she kept on trying
But she couldn't catch up to the bird that was flying.

And as she was running, the hen met a bike.
And she said to it, "Bicycle, you seem like
A lending-a-hand-to-a-friend kind of guy.
Will you help me catch up to that bird in the sky?"

"Sure!" The bike answered. "Hop onto my seat!"
So the hen hopped up, and they zoomed down the street.
They rode and they rode for a long, long while.
They rode and they rode, mile after mile.
The bicycle's bell went RING-RING RING-RING
But the bird was too far away to hear a thing.

They didn't stop riding, they kept on trying,
But they couldn't catch up to the bird that was flying.

Too tired to continue, the bicycle slowed.
"What's faster," the hen wondered, "than this bike I just rode?"

That's right! A car!

As the hen continued on, she came to a car
And she said, "I need to go fast and go far.
I need to catch up to that bird in the sky.
Can you give me a ride? Will you give it a try?"

"Get in!" said the car. "Let's get moving fast."
So the hen jumped inside, and they stepped on the gas.
They drove and they drove, for a long, long while.
They drove and they drove, mile after mile.

BEEP BEEP HONK HONK went the horn of the car.
But the bird couldn't hear it. She was much too far.
They didn't stop driving, they kept on trying
But they couldn't catch up to the bird that was flying.

Finally, the car could go no more.
So they stopped, and the hen hopped out the door.
"This car was helpful, and took me far.
But what is faster than a car?"

That's right! A train!

As she continued her chase, the hen met a train
And she said, "Here's the story: I had some grain,
And I didn't share it with a poor hungry bird,
And now I need to catch up with her. And you are the third
Vehicle I'm trying, because I need to go fast.
Can you help me catch her, Train?" the hen asked.

"Sure!" the train answered. "Jump right in!"
So the hen climbed inside the train's engine.
They chugged and they chugged, for a long, long while.
They chugged and they chugged, mile after mile.
CLICKITY-CLACK went the train down the track
But the bird couldn't hear it. She didn't look back.

They didn't stop chugging, they kept on trying.
But they couldn't catch up to the bird that was flying.

The train was quite fast, but not fast enough.
He started to slow, to huff and to puff.
"I MUST catch that bird and give her some grain!
But what," the hen wondered, "is faster than a train?"

That's right! An airplane!

The hen met an airplane, and she asked, "Could you please,
Take me up in the air, over the mountains and trees?
There's a bird up there, who's hungry for grain.
Will you help me catch her?" the hen asked the plane.

The plane said, "Get in. And I'll help get you there."
So the hen hopped inside, and they flew through the air.
They flew and they flew, for a long, long while.
They flew and they flew, mile after mile.
The propellers spun quickly, the engine roared loud
As they sped through the air, through the fluffy white clouds.
And suddenly...

The bird was right there!
Flying right next to them, up in the air!

The hen was ecstatic! Now she could finally feed
The little bird with food from her large plate of seed.
She handed her a bag filled with grains of wheat
And she said, "I'm so sorry I didn't let you eat.
I'm sorry I tried to keep it all for myself.
There's plenty for both of us, so eat in good health.
From now on, I think that the right thing to do
Is to share my food with others, and especially with you."

What's in the Package?

Nati's Abba bought him a present
Wrapped in shiny purple paper.
He asked Nati to guess what's inside.
Can you help Nati decide?

– Maybe you bought me a menorah to light!
With eight silver branches, one for each night.

– No, Nati. Kislev was long ago.
It isn't winter. There isn't snow.
But when Chanukah time
comes around again,
I'll buy you a menorah,
im yirtzeh Hashem.

–Is it apples and honey, delicious and sweet?

– No, Nati. That is what we eat
On Rosh Hashana. But that's not today.
Keep guessing. I don't want to give it away.

– Oy, Abba! I can hardly wait!
Is it an *essrog,* on a silver plate?

– No. Sukkos is in Tishrei. Rosh Hashana is, too.
Keep guessing what I bought for you!

– Maybe you bought me a treat for lunch.
Nice round matzahs, that crackle and crunch?

– Oh, Nati. You'd have to wait nearly a year
For Pesach, in Nissan, to be near.

– Oh! I know what's inside!
That package has the shape
Of a king costume.
A crown and cape!

– No, Nati. But when Purim
comes around
If you want, I'll buy you
a cape and crown.

– Oy, Abba. I can't wait one more minute!
Please open the package and show me what's in it!

– OK, Nati. If you've given up,
Here's what's inside....

A washing cup!

You fill it up every night before bed,
And in the morning, after *modeh ani* is said,
You wash *netilas yadaim*—three times on each hand.
And then your day can start as planned.

– Wow! I love to have mitzvos to do!
Thank you, Abba! Thank you, thank you!
This present is special, precious and dear.
And I'll use it with pride, every day of the year!

Rain from Heaven

One morning Chani noticed that
Everything outside was wet.
The streets, the trees,
The whole neighborhood!
So she zipped up her coat
And pulled on her hood.
Chani was happy there was rain
But she was dry now,
And dry she hoped to remain.

Down the street hurried Rabbi Rand
An umbrella clutched in his right hand.
He was on his way to learn and pray.
Even this downpour couldn't keep him away.
Rabbi Rand was happy there was rain.
But he was dry now,
And dry he hoped to remain.

Across the street little Moshe stood
With no umbrella or a hood.
He could not go out in such a state.
He would simply have to wait.
Moshe was happy there was rain.
But he was dry now,
And dry he hoped to remain.

A neighborhood cat hid under a car.
She could not venture very far.
Although she was hungry and wanted a meal,
All she could do now
Was huddle next to a wheel.
The cat was happy there was rain.
But she was dry now,
And dry she hoped to remain.

Baby Esti was under a big plastic cover
Over her stroller, being pushed by her mother.
The raindrops tapped against the plastic,
And Baby Esti thought it sounded fantastic!
Esti was happy there was rain.
But she was dry now,
And dry she hoped to remain.

Up on her balcony, Mrs. Fine
Was quickly pulling clothes
Off the laundry line.
She had just finished washing and drying them.
And she didn't want to have to do it again.
Mrs. Fine was happy there was rain.
But her laundry was dry,
And dry she hoped it'd remain.

But despite the rain falling hard,
Chani noticed something in her yard.
A beautiful flower, bright and red,
With big wet raindrops hitting its head.

Chani thought to herself, "This rain is good.
But that poor little flower has no hood.
No one I saw today liked to get wet,
And that flower does not like it either, I bet."

So taking great care not to bend it or break it
She placed plastic over the flower to make it
A little hood, and then she tied it below
So it would stay in place when the wind would blow.

Chani came home from school that day
With rain still pouring, the sky still gray.
She ran to the garden to check on the flower
She had covered to protect it from getting a shower.

But Chani was shocked and surprised to find
That though she had tried to be helpful and kind,
Her flower was drooping, it looked so sad,
And she asked it, "What happened? I thought you'd be glad
To be kept nice and dry. But you don't look well.
How can I help you feel better? Please tell."

The flower answered, "Let me explain.
I love to get wet. I need the rain.
I was sad because no matter how hard I'd try
To drink up the water, I just stayed dry.
People run inside when there's a storm
So they can stay nice and dry. and warm.
But flowers love to get wetter and wetter.
If you let me get wet, I will feel so much better."

That evening Chani peeked into the yard.
The rain was still coming down very hard.
But through the mist Chani saw very clearly
The bright red flower she loved so dearly,
Dancing in the breeze. And it was quite plain
It was happy to be dripping wet in the rain.

The Special Treats

One day, a bunch of candies went
Looking for some fun.
A chocolate bar, some lollipops,
Sucking candies, and some gum.

They came to a tall building.
On the first floor,
They knocked on the door.

The candies called out:
"We are candies, delicious and sweet.
Open the door, and come have a treat!"

Three children opened the door and said:
"Candy is tasty; that is true.
But our teeth will get cativities
If we eat you."

The candies were sad, but they didn't fret.

They'd find some children
Who'd want them, yet.

They climbed up the stairs.
On the second floor,
They knocked on the door.

The candies called out:
"We are candies, delicious and sweet.
Open the door, and come have a treat!"

Two children opened the door and said:
"We only eat healthful food,
Like milk, fruits, and bread.
Please find someone else
To eat you instead."

The candies were trying to stay upbeat.
They'd find someone else
Who would want them to eat.

78

They climbed up the stairs.
On the third floor,
They knocked on the door.

The candies called out:
"We are candies, delicious and sweet.
Open the door, and come have a treat!"

Three children opened the door and said:
"Candy before dinner might
Ruin our appetite.
Now is not a time for sweets,
When we are about to eat."

The candies left, with great dismay.
Wouldn't any children let them stay?

They climbed the stairs.
On the fourth floor,
They knocked on the door.

The candies called out:
"We are candies, delicious and sweet.
Open the door, and come have a treat!"

The children opened the door and said:
"Candy is great, but not for every day.
But, we are going to let you stay.
Climb into the cupboard
And wait a while.
Tomorrow is Shabbos,"
They said with a smile.

After Shabbos had arrived,
Mommy took the candy out to divide.
She took out special bags,
And in each one
She put some
Chocolate,
lollipops,
sucking candy,
and gum.

The Best Place for an Elephant

In a beautiful jungle full of flowers and trees,
Lion and tigers, and swinging monkeys,
Lived Olly the elephant, a fanciful dreamer,
Who left the jungle one day to board a large steamer.

The jungle was boring. He was there every day,
And he was looking for a place more interesting to play.

So with excitement he planned an adventurous trip,
Packed his trunk, said goodbye and boarded the ship.
Quickly, the ship began to sail. Olly felt a thrill from his trunk to his tail.
The waves rocked the boat gently, to and fro, as they sailed farther and farther
From Olly's home.

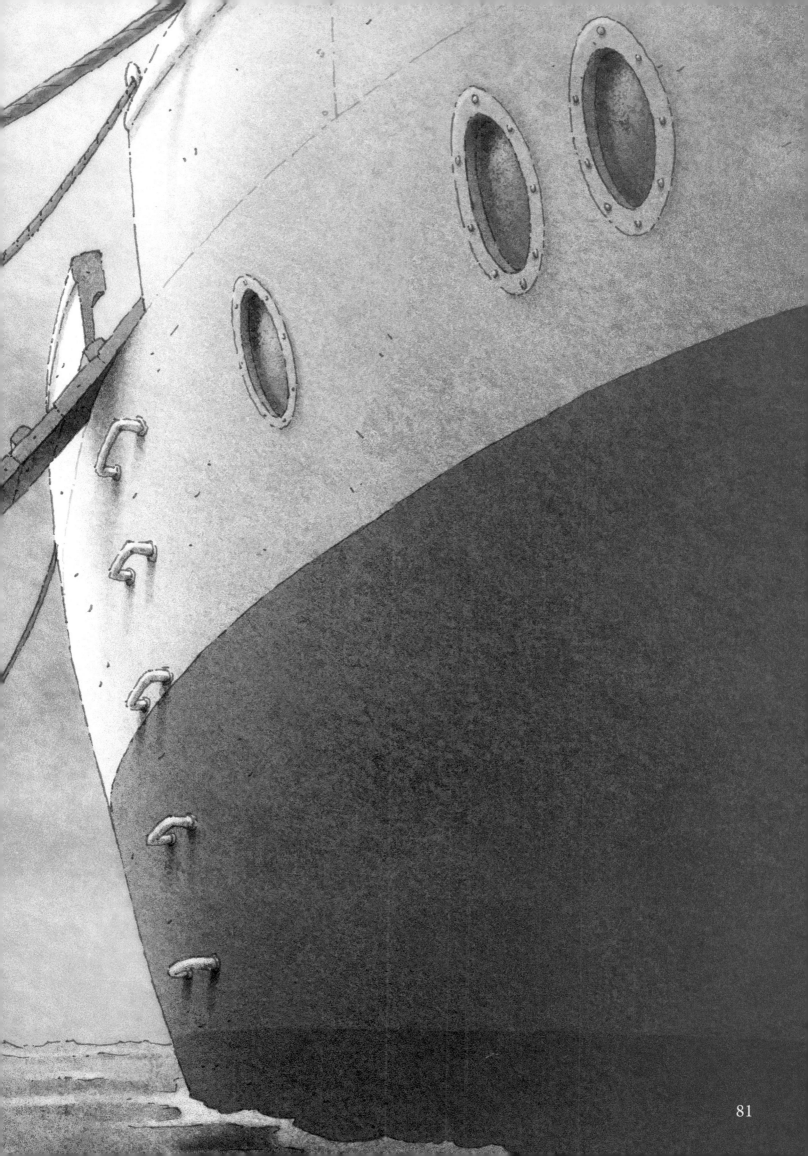

Suddenly...

The boat came to a stop in a strange new place.
Olly looked around with excitement on his face.
This place was different, unusual, new!
But there was a little problem or two.

The ground was frozen, covered in snow.
Olly shivered as the wind began to blow.
It was so cold, people built houses from ice!
How could anyone think this place was nice?"

Olly looked around, and standing right there
Was a large, white, furry polar bear.
Surprised, Olly said, "I don't understand
How you live in this place and are able to stand

This incredible cold. I'm chilled to the bone.
How can you call this frigid wasteland home?"

The polar bear answered, "With Hashem's design,
I'm never cold. I feel just fine.
I have nice, warm fur—fluffy and soft.
It keeps the cold away, and water rolls off.

Olly realized without a warm coat,
He could not live in the arctic
So he returned to the boat.

Once again, the ship set sail and Olly felt a thrill from his trunk to his tail.
The waves rocked the boat gently, to and fro, as they sailed farther and farther
From Olly's home.

83

Suddenly...

The boat came to a stop in a strange new place.
Olly looked around with excitement on his face.
This place was different, unusual, new!
But once again, there was a problem or two.

Everywhere he looked was just sand and sky.
No trees, grass or water. It was totally dry.
He was tired and thirsty, and itchy with sand.
How could any animal survive in this land?!

Olly looked around, and was taken aback
When he saw a camel, with a hump on his back.

Olly said, "I don't understand
How you live in this hot place,
Covered in sand.

With no food and no water. No shade to cool down.
What a terrible place," Olly said with a frown.

The camel answered, "With Hashem's design
I'm not hot or thirsty. I feel just fine.
When I have food and drink I consume great amounts
So I'll have what I need to live, when it counts.

This hump on my back
stores what I need
For when I can't find
water, or a place to feed".

Olly realized his trip
would be very short
With no water in the desert,
So he returned to the port.

Once again, the ship set sail
And Olly felt a thrill
From his trunk to his tail.
The waves rocked the boat
Gently, to and fro,
As they sailed farther and farther
From Olly's home.

Suddenly...

The boat stopped in the middle of the ocean,
And Olly the elephant got the notion
To dive into the water.
What a great place to see!
And he won't get too hot
Or too cold or thirsty.

So down, down he dived to this interesting place
With a look of excitement on his face.
And oh! The things he saw below!
The ocean floor was quite a show!
Fish of all colors, rocks of all sizes.
A place full of new things,
And full of surprises.

But Olly soon became aware
Of one small problem...
THERE WAS NO AIR!

Olly said to a fish nearby,
"I can't even begin to try
To figure out why you don't leave
This place where there isn't even air to breathe!"

The fish answered, "With Hashem's design,
I don't need air and I feel just fine.
We both need oxygen, that is true.
But I get mine in a different way than you do.
My gills filter the water to give me what I need...
But you better get to the surface, so you can breathe!"

Back on the boat, Olly now knew
Exactly what he needed to do.
"I'll sail back to the jungle,
The place I belong.
All those other places
I tried felt wrong.

Hashem created me
A certain way,
For a certain place.
And I'm returning today!

In the jungle it is not too hot
It's not too cold, and there's a lot
Of water to drink, to bathe in and spray.
There's air to breathe,
and friends to play!"

Back in the jungle Olly celebrated
His return to the place
For which he was created.
With a trunk full of water
Spraying up in the air,

He said, "From now on,
I'm not going anywhere.
This is the best place for me
And I never will roam.
There's no place like the jungle.
There's no place like home."

Mixed-up Moshe

Do you know this boy?
His name is Moshe,
And he can draw anything!
A lion, a puppy, a vase full of flowers,
Or a tree with a tire swing.
He can draw airplanes, trains, trucks and cars.
A kite, or a bunch of balloons,
A juggling clown, a brave fireman,
Or an astronaut on the moon!

Today his friends are making requests,
Asking Moshe to draw
The things they like best.

The first request came from Ari.
"Draw a car on a bridge, and a boat in the sea."

Moshe's pencil was at the ready,
He drew the picture, sure and steady.
The drawing was done before very long.
And here it is! But what looks wrong?

"A bridge is not the place for a boat.
It cannot move if it cannot float.
And look at this car," said Ari, "I think
That a car in the water would probably sink."

"Oh, you're right!" Said Moshe.
"It's all mixed-up.
If you get me more paper,
I'll fix it right up."

"Thank you, Moshe. This one looks right."
And Ari ran off with his drawing held tight.

The next request came from Elchanan.
"Draw a father walking to school with his son."

Moshe's pencil was at the ready,
He drew the picture, sure and steady.
The drawing was done before very long.
And here it is! But what looks wrong?

"A boy who's big and a
father who's small?
That doesn't look right
to me at all!"

"Oh, you're right!"
Said Moshe.
"It's all mixed-up.
If you get me more paper,
I'll fix it right up."

"Thank you, Moshe.
This one looks right."
And Elchanan ran off
with his drawing held tight.

Soon, Yaakov came with a request for
Fish in a river, and a horse on the shore.

Moshe's pencil was at the ready,
He drew the picture, sure and steady.
The drawing was done before very long.
And here it is! But something looks wrong!

"There's fish in the grass,
and horses in the sky!
But fish need water, and
horses don't fly!"

"Oh, you're right!"
Said Moshe.
"It's all mixed-up.
If you get me more paper,
I'll fix it right up."

"Thank you, Moshe. This one looks right."
And Yaakov ran off with his drawing held tight.

Along came Chaim and said, "I would like
A picture of a boy with a bike."

Moshe's pencil was at the ready,
He drew the picture, sure and steady.
The drawing was done before very long.
And here it is! But what looks wrong?

"This boy has wheels
instead of feet!
He would roll away,
right down the street!
And triangle wheels
on a mountain bike?
You couldn't ride that.
You'd have to hike."

"Oh, you're right!"
Said Moshe.
"It's all mixed-up.
If you get me more paper,
I'll fix it right up."

"Thank you, Moshe.
This one looks right."
And Chaim ran off
with his drawing held tight.

Next came Micha with a request
For the drawing he thought would be best.
"Can you draw a picture of my Zeidy
Writing a special letter to me?"

Moshe's pencil was at the ready,
He drew the picture, sure and steady.
The drawing was done before very long.
And here it is! But what looks wrong?

"A fork for writing?
I don't understand.
There should be a pencil
in his hand!"

"Oh, you're right!"
said Moshe.
"It's all mixed-up.
If you get me more paper,
I'll fix it right up."

But as Moshe started
To fix his drawing,
His eyes started drooping,
And he started yawning.
He laid his head down
Right there on the table.
To stay awake any longer,
He just wasn't able.

So maybe YOU can help make the picture better!
Can you draw a Zeidy writing a letter?